This Little Tiger book belongs to:

_____

_____

_____

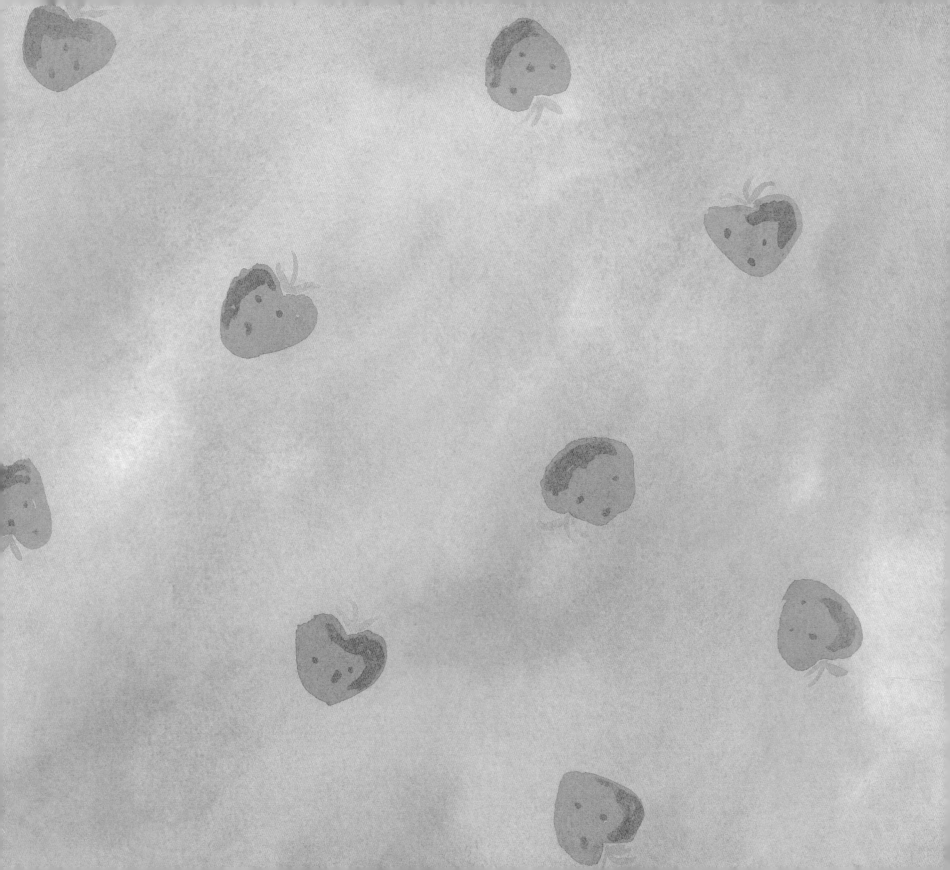

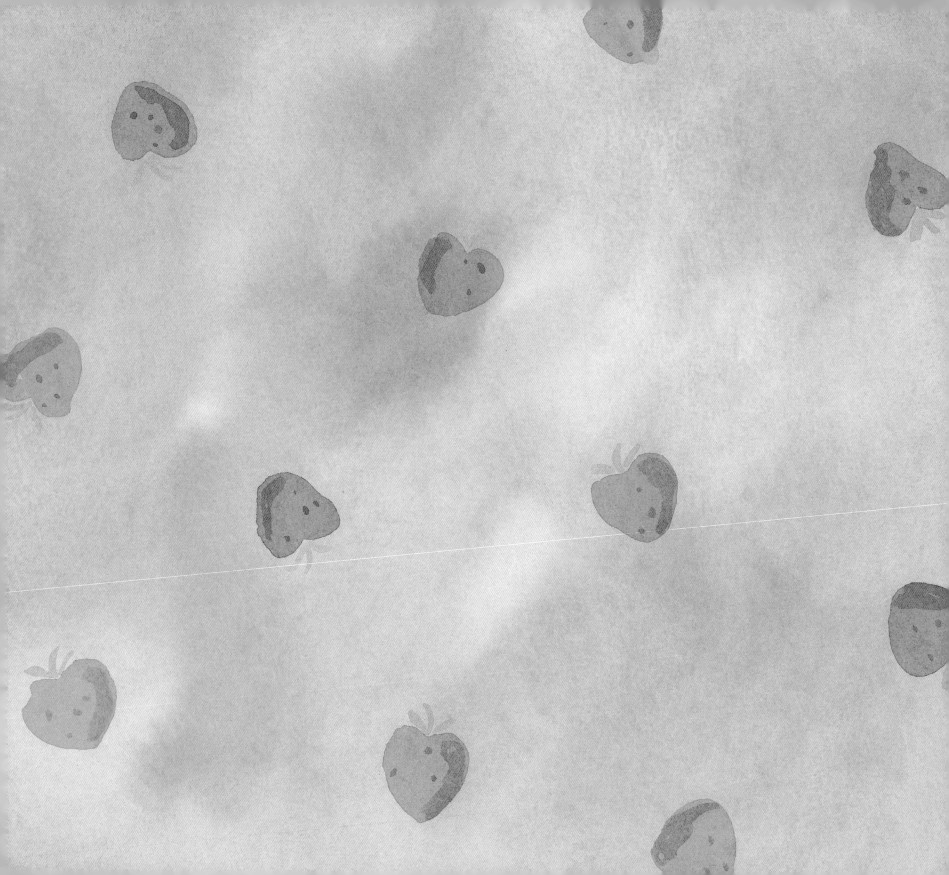

For my good friend
Elaine
CF

For Grandma,
with love
JM

LITTLE TIGER PRESS LTD,
an imprint of the Little Tiger Group
1 The Coda Centre, 189 Munster Road, London SW6 6AW
www.littletiger.co.uk

First published in Great Britain 2003
This edition published 2003

ISBN 978-1-85430-902-0

A CIP catalogue record for this book is available
from the British Library

Printed in China • LTP/1400/1877/0417

1 3 5 7 9 10 8 6 4 2

Night-Night, Poppy!

written by

Claire Freedman

illustrated by

Jane Massey

LiTTLE TiGER

LONDON

It was bedtime, but Poppy couldn't find her favourite bear, Growly Ted. She'd looked everywhere.

Mummy had to tuck her in
with Quacky Duck instead.
"Night-night, Poppy, night-night,
Quacky Duck," said Mummy.
"Night-night, Mummy and
Quacky Duck," said Poppy.
"Quack-quack!" quacked Quacky Duck.

Poppy would have fallen fast
asleep right then. But OH NO!
The bed didn't feel quite right.
It felt too cold. So Poppy went
to find Furry Cat.

"Night-night, Quacky Duck
and Furry Cat," said Poppy.
"Miaow," purred Furry Cat.
"Quack-quack," quacked
Quacky Duck.

Poppy would have fallen fast asleep that
very minute. But OH NO! The bed STILL
didn't feel quite right. It felt too empty.
Out Poppy climbed to look for Hooty Owl.

"Night-night," Poppy told Hooty Owl, Furry Cat
and Quacky Duck.

"Too-whit too-whoo," hooted Hooty Owl.

"Miaow," purred Furry Cat.

"Quack-quack," quacked Quacky Duck. "Quack!"

Poppy would have fallen asleep in a flash.

But OH NO! Now the bed felt all wrong.

It seemed too draughty.

Where had Dimple Dog got to?

Poppy found him downstairs, behind the curtains.

"Night-night, Dimple Dog and
Hooty Owl," said Poppy. "Night-night,
Furry Cat and Quacky Duck."
"Woof-woof," barked Dimple Dog.
"Too-whit too-whoo," hooted Hooty Owl.
"Miaow," purred Furry Cat.

Quacky Duck didn't say a word.
He was already fast asleep.

Poppy would have fallen fast asleep too.
But OH NO! Now the bed covers felt too loose.
Poppy crept out to find Woolly Lamb.

"Night-night, everyone," said Poppy.
"Baa-baa," bleated Woolly Lamb.
"Woof-woof," barked Dimple Dog.
"Too-whit too-whoo," hooted Hooty Owl.
"Miaow," purred Furry Cat.
"Quack-quack," quacked Quacky Duck,
 who'd woken up again with all the noise.

Now Poppy would have fallen fast
asleep in an instant. But OH NO!
She just couldn't get comfy.
The pillow felt all lumpy.
"What's under here?" said Poppy.
"Oh, so that's where you've been
hiding, silly Growly Ted!"

Then Poppy put
Quacky Duck
back in the toy box.

She propped
Furry Cat back
up on his shelf.

She put Hooty Owl
back under
the bed.

And she carried
Dimple Dog
and Woolly Lamb
back downstairs.

Then Poppy and Growly Ted settled
down together under the covers.
"Night-night, Growly Ted," yawned
Poppy.
"Grrr!" growled Growly Ted.
And Poppy fell fast asleep. OH YES!
Because the bed felt just right.

And Growly Ted
would have fallen fast asleep
that same second too.
But OH NO! . . .

Suddenly the bed
was far too full!
"Grrrr!"

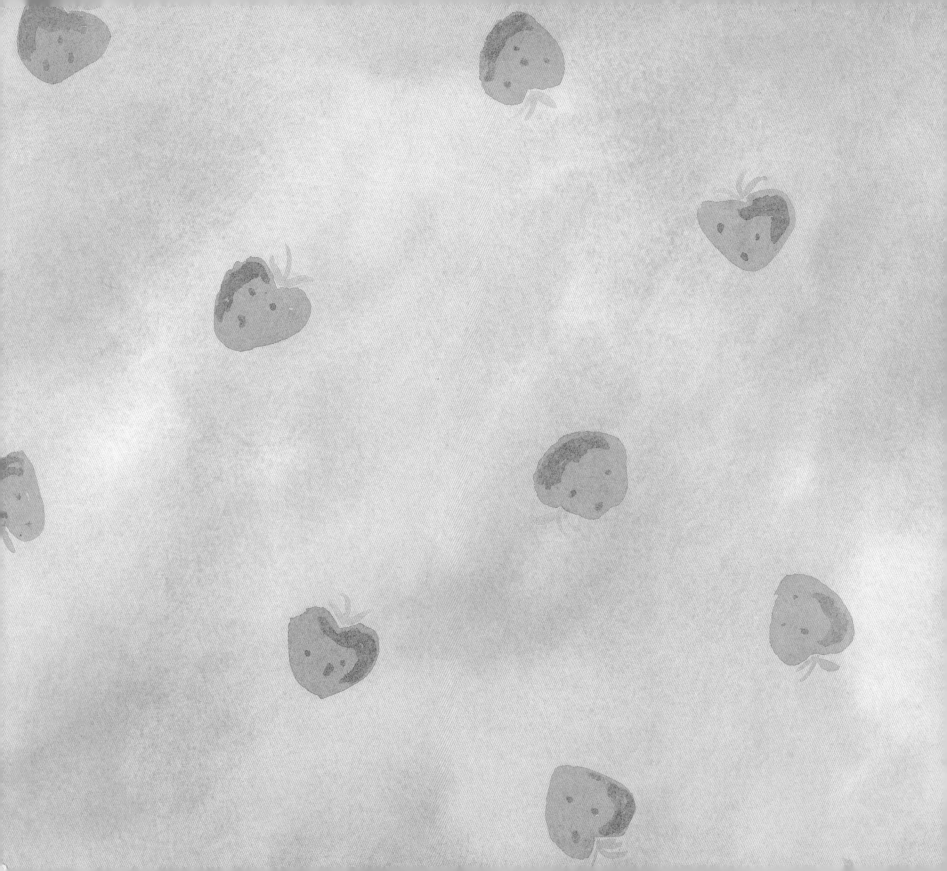

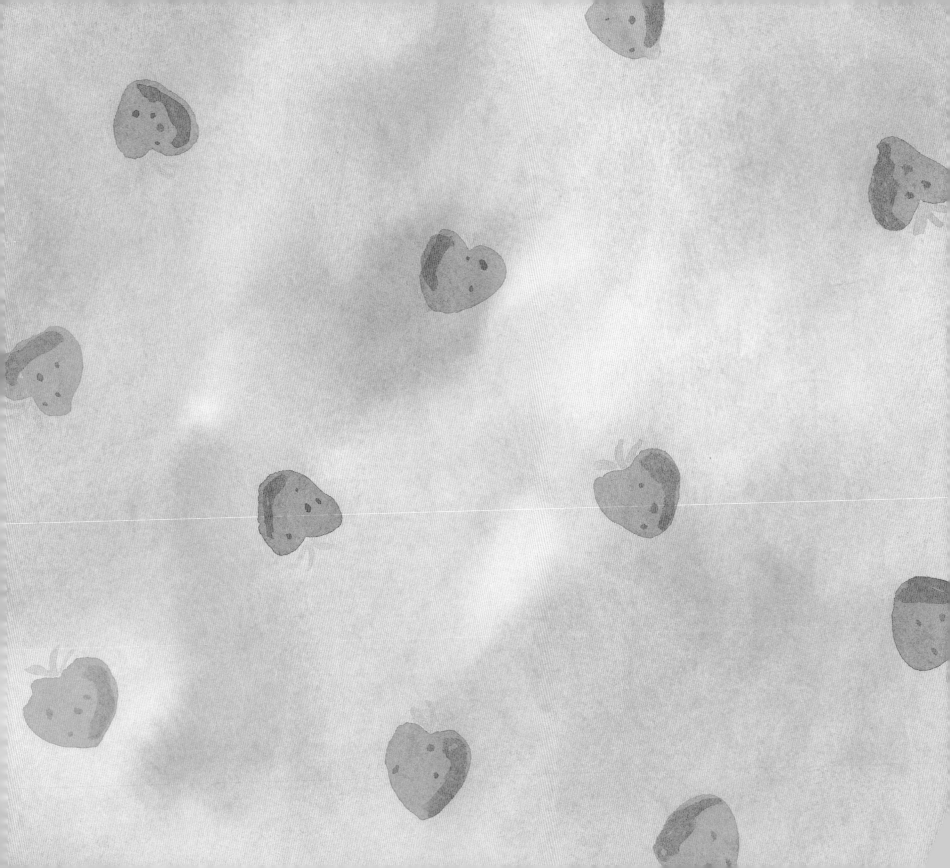

More fabulous books from Little Tiger Press!

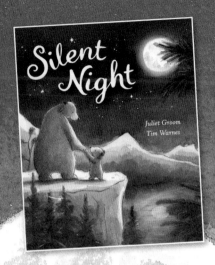

Silent Night

Juliet Groom
Tim Warnes

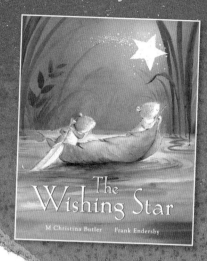

The Wishing Star

M Christina Butler   Frank Endersby

Time to Sleep, Alfie Bear!

Catherine Walters

Don't Wake the Bear, Hare!

Steve Smallman
Caroline Pedler

The Very Noisy Night

Diana Hendry
Illustrated by Jane Chapman

Under the Silvery Moon

COLLEEN McKEOWN

For information regarding any of the above titles
or for our catalogue, please contact us:
Little Tiger Press, 1 The Coda Centre, 189 Munster Road, London SW6 6AW
Tel: 020 7385 6333 • Email: contact@littletiger.co.uk • www.littletiger.co.uk
Image taken from *Silent Night* copyright © Tim Warnes 2010
Visit Tim Warnes at www.ChapmanandWarnes.com